ONE
DAY

박노해 사진에세이
01

하
루

O N E
D A Y

PARK NOHAE PHOTO ESSAY 01

느린걸음

나는 하루 하루 살아왔다
감동하고 감사하고 감내하며

I have ever lived day by day
I am touched, give thanks, endure

CONTENTS

Preface

A Long Day's Life · 17

Photography

Drawing Water at Daybreak · **26** Every Morning Flowers · **30** Sunlight in a Teacup · **32**

Dawn Market in Khartoum · **36** An Old Teak Wood Bridge · **38** Fishing in Inle Lake · **42**

The Sower of Seeds · **44** Girls Picking Cotton · **46** Women by the Ganges River · **48**

Barley Harvest on the Tibetan Plateau · **50** Bolivian Miners Returning Home · **54**

Dazzling Time above Ground · **56** A Dignified Return · **58**

Harvesting Potatoes on the Andes Plateau · **60** Talking in an Earth-Roofed Yard · **64**

Off We Go, Yaks, back to our Home on the Grasslands · **66** A Mother of Four · **70**

Brother's Barbershop · **72** The True Education of 'the Playing Teacher' · **74**

Like a Barefooted Messi · **78** Splashing about with Water Buffalo · **80**

A Girl Growing Trees · **82** The Road across the Desert to the Marketplace · **86**

The Work of Hill-Tribe Women · **88** Vigor in a Traditional Market · **90**

Q'ero Village General Assembly · **92** 'Reading while Walking' in the Wilderness · **94**

Greetings after Finishing the Day's Work · **98** Meditation in Silence · **100**

When Father Comes Home · **102** Diving into a Flowing River · **106**

Washing Clothes in the Irrawaddy River · **108** A Rajasthan Woman at Sunset · **112**

Supper Table on Earth · **116** Going Home by Bicycle · **118** Time to Drink Chai · **120**

Setting out Again at Dawn · **122**

Biography · **130**

Books · **132**

서문

긴 하루의 생 · **9**

작품

여명에 물을 긷다 · **26** 아침마다 꽃 · **30** 찻잔에 햇살을 담아 · **32**

카르툼 새벽 시장 · **36** 오래된 티크 나무 다리 · **38** 인레 호수의 고기잡이 · **42**

씨앗을 심는 사람 · **44** 목화송이를 따는 소녀 · **46** 갠지스강의 여인들 · **48**

티베트 고원의 보리 수확 · **50** 볼리비아 광부들의 퇴근길 · **54**

눈부신 지상의 시간 · **56** 당당한 귀항 · **58** 안데스 고원의 감자 수확 · **60**

흙지붕 마당의 담소 · **64** 가자 야크들아, 초원의 집으로 · **66** 네 아이의 엄마 · **70**

형제 이발소 · **72** '날라리 선생'의 참교육 · **74** 맨발의 메시처럼 · **78**

물소와 함께 물장구 · **80** 나무를 키우는 소녀 · **82** 사막을 건너 장터로 가는 길 · **86**

고산족 여인들의 작품 · **88** 재래시장의 생기 · **90** 께로족 마을 총회 · **92**

황야의 '걷는 독서' · **94** 하루 일을 마치는 인사 · **98** 고요 속의 묵상 · **100**

아빠가 돌아올 때 · **102** 흐르는 강물에 몸을 담고 · **106** 이라와디강가의 빨래 · **108**

석양빛의 라자스탄 여인 · **112** 지상의 저녁 밥상 · **116**

자전거를 타고 귀가할 때 · **118** 짜이를 마시는 시간 · **120**

다시 길 떠나는 새벽 · **122**

약력 · **127**

저서 · **132**

긴 하루의 생

긴 하루였다. 나의 어린 시절은.

이른 아침 새소리에 눈을 뜨면, 붉게 물든 감 잎사귀와 시든 꽃잎이 떨어진 마당을 쓰는 건 나의 일이었다. 대빗자루 자국이 난 정갈한 흙마당에 햇살이 빛나면 아침밥을 짓던 어머니가 마루에 나를 앉히고서 '애썼다. 차암 곱지야' 미소를 지었다. 물동이를 인 누나 뒤를 종종종 따라 샘터에 다녀와 찬물로 얼굴을 씻고 학교에 갈 때면, 키 큰 수수와 해바라기가 선 논둑길을 걸어가는 내 머리 위로 고추잠자리와 참새들이 나를 놀리며 따라다녔다. 교실에 앉아 창 너머로 흐르는 흰 구름을 바라보고 길 떠나는 기러기 떼를 바라보고, 작은 도서관에서 허기진 배보다 더 허기진 꿈으로 까만 씨알 같은 활자들을 읽으며 시간도 잊은 채 가슴 콩닥이는 모험에 빠져들었다. 교문을 나서 장터를 지나 여기저기 돌아다니다 과꽃이랑 산국화를 꺾어 들고 집에 오면, 암탉이 낳은 따뜻한 달걀을 거두어 바구니에 담아두고 장날이 오기를 손꼽아 보았다. 염소를 몰고 나가 방죽 풀밭에 묶어둔 채 동무들이랑 바닷

물에 뛰어들어 놀다가 전어랑 숭어를 잡아 갈댓잎에 꿰어 들고 와 얼른 부엌에 던져두곤 다시 뛰어나갔다. 정미소 마당에서 호박죽 내기가 걸린 형과 누나들 배구 경기를 소리 질러 응원하고 기마놀이 닭싸움 공차기 구슬치기를 하느라 해가 저무는 줄도 몰랐다. '얘야 저녁 다 됐다, 밥 먹고 내일 또 놀으렴' 골목마다 엄마가 부르는 소리에 하나둘 저녁연기 피어오르는 집으로 돌아가 밥을 먹고서 숙제를 하는 둥 마는 둥 하고는 연필에 침을 묻혀 가며 일기를 쓰다가, 좋아하는 소녀에게 몰래몰래 편지를 쓰고 지우며 비밀스레 가슴앓이 하는 밤이었다. 호롱불 아래 묵주기도를 하는 엄마 무릎에 누워 깜빡 잠이 들었다가 오줌이 마려워 일어나 어둠에 빛나는 총총한 별들을 바라보다 선듯한 바람에 으스스 돌아와 이불 속으로 파고들어 세상모르게 단잠에 들었던 날들.

그 시절 우리의 하루는 긴 하루였다. 가난도 불운도 어쩌지 못한 충만한 하루하루였다. 달콤하고 기름진 것도 없고 재미난 기계와 텔레비전도 없고 스마트폰도 컴퓨터도 없었지만, 그 결여와 심심함이 오히려 인간적 풍요와 우애와 관심을 북돋고 자기 앞가림하는 능력과 더불어 사는 능력을 키워주던 시절. 여백과 여운이 넘치는 유장한 시간은 나를 주체적으로 살아 움직이게 하는 넉넉한 무대가 되고, 상상력과 창조성과 이야기를 낳게 하고, 어른들 몰래몰래 아찔한 모험과 탐험의 열정을 불태우게 하던 시절. 그토록 풍요로운 가난과 그토록 빛나던 긴 하루가 우리에겐 살아있었다.

아 그러나 좋았던 시절만이 긴 하루가 아니었다. 상처와 고통의 시절도 긴 하루였다. 분단과 독재로 내 조국이 어려움에 처했을 때, 슬

품과 분노로 고뇌하고 노동하고 독서하고 조직하고 투쟁하던 나의 청년 시절 또한 긴 하루였다. 전쟁 같은 철야 노동의 시간, 서럽고 억울한 천대와 차별의 시간, 무력한 사랑의 패배와 좌절의 뼈저린 시간, 사로잡힌 짐승처럼 피 흘리던 고문장의 시간, 감옥 독방 속 시퍼런 수의에 갇힌 무기수의 시간, 그리고 자유의 몸이 되어서도 긴장과 공포 어린 분쟁 현장을 누빈 시간, 사막과 광야와 만년설산 고원 길의 막막한 시간. 나의 생은 참으로 긴 하루 또 하루의 날들이었다.

해가 길어지고 해가 짧아지고, 지나온 날보다 남은 날이 많지 않고, 인생의 몇 단계 문을 통과하고 나면 알게 되리라. 누구에게나 어린 시절은 아이가 자라듯 '훌쩍' 지나가고 찬란하던 청춘도 '번쩍' 하고 지나가지만, 그 무정한 세월도 어찌지 못하는 '긴 하루'만은 내 안에 살아 있음을. 그 많은 하루하루 가운데 오로지 긴 하루만이 그립고 눈물 나는 기억으로 남아있고, 그 긴 하루만이 내가 진정 살아있었던 날이었음을. 더 많이 소유하고 더 높이 오르려는 경쟁과 질주로 흘러가는 덧없는 인생 가운데 한 사람에게 이번 생의 결실로 주어지는 건 그 긴 하루의 날들이 아니겠는가. 반복되는 일상 속에서도 그 긴 하루가 생생히 살아있어 나를 다시 일어서게 하고 내 등을 밀어주며 앞으로 나아가게 하는 힘이 아니겠는가.

지난 20여 년간 나는 지상의 가장 멀고 높고 깊은 마을을 찾아다녔다. 지구시대의 유랑자로 지도에도 없는 마을을 찾아다녔다. 그랬다. 이 여정의 목적지는 처음부터 여기였다. 하루, 긴 하루, 다른 하루.

'하루'. 참으로 평범하고도 경이롭고, 흔하고도 무서운 말이 '하루'다. 하나의 물방울이 온 하늘을 담고 있듯 하루 속에는 영원이 깃들어 있는 일일일생一日一生의 하루이기 때문이다. 그러나 오늘 우리의 하루는 저 영원과 신성이 끊어진 물질에 잠긴 시간이 되고 말았다. 지금 시대는 돈이 없이는 살 수 없고 돈이 있어도 삶이 없는 시대가 되었다. 그로부터 인생은 늘 '준비'에서 또 다른 '준비'로 흘러가고, 지금 여기의 삶은 미래를 위해 참고 견디는 고통의 연속이 되고 말았다. 인류 역사에서 오직 현대의 인간만이 존재하지도 않는 '미래'를 위해 '오늘'뿐인 삶을 유보시킨다. 그러나 우리에겐 미래가 없다. 오직 희망만이 있을 뿐.

내가 나 자신의 하루를 살지 않는다면 무언가 내 하루를 앗아가고 만다. 내가 나 자신을 연구하지 않는다면 누군가 나를 연구해 자원으로 써먹어 간다. 모든 악의 세력이 지배하려는 최후의 목적지, 세계화된 자본권력이 점령하고자 하는 최후의 영토는 나 개인들의 내면과 하루 일과가 아닌가. 그리하여 우리의 내면과 일상은 소리 없는 전쟁터다. 여기가 이 시대의 최전선이다. 나의 내면과 일상에서는 지금 '악의 신비'와 '선의 도약'이 투쟁하고 있다. 선도 악도, 사랑도 탐욕도, 아름다움도 비루함도 나의 내면과 일상에서 시작되고 그것으로 귀결된다.

이 문명의 근원 독점Radical Monopoly 시스템에 얽혀든 채 하루하루 나의 무력감을 절감하며 살지라도, 그래도 우리는 진정한 나를 찾아 좋은 삶을 살아내며 좋은 세상을 향해 나아가는 생의 분투를 포기할 수 없다. 거듭 실패하고 좌절할지라도 다시 시작하고 꾸준히 밀어 가는 것, 그것이 날마다 내게 주어지는 평범한 하루하루의 위대함이다.

나는 그 하루의 무게를 알고 있다. 군사독재에 맞서다 안기부 지하 밀실에 끌려가 고문을 당할 때였다. 50여 명이 24시간 교대로 자행

하는 고문장의 하루하루는 의지도, 생각도, 투지도 작용할 수 없는 오직 비명만이 가득한 새하얀 시간이었다. 그들이 요구하는 건 간단했다. '단 한 명만 불어라!' 그러나 만약 내가 한 명의 동지를 불고 나면 그들은 최후까지 밀어붙일 것이었다. '하나만 더. 하나만 더!'

그것을 뚫고 나가는 나의 주문은 단 한 마디였다. '하루만 더. 하루만 더! 나 여기까지 살아왔는데, 그래 오늘 하루가 나의 끝이다, 내 생의 마지막 하루다. 그러니 오늘 하루만 더! 죽는 최후의 순간까지 하루만 더!' 그렇게 24일이 지났던 것 같다.

인생이건 역사건, 결정적 대목은 이 한 마디가 아닐까. '하나만 더'에 맞서 '하루만 더'. 사람은 '하나만 더'에 타협할 때, 그 하나가 꺾일 때, 하나하나 결국 자신을 다 내어주게 되는 것이니. 그리하여 나의 사명은 단 하루다. 우리 희망도 사랑도 혁명도 단 하루다. '하나만 더에 맞서 하루만 더'. 그렇게 나는 오늘도 하루하루 첫마음의 길을 걸어갈 뿐이다.

수천 년의 하루가 터무늬로 이어져온 저 멀고 높은 지구마을들을 걸어 다니다 첨단 도시로 돌아올 때면, 나는 아득한 생의 시차를 잃곤 한다. 너무 빠른 속도와 폭포 같은 정보 속에서 누구나 다 알고 똑똑해진 시대다. 그럴수록 삶에서 가장 중요한 어떤 능력이 고갈되어가고 있음을 느낀다. 그것은 감동할 줄 아는 힘과 감사하는 힘 그리고 감내하는 힘이다.

살아있는 인간에게 있어 오늘 하루는 반복되는 일상임과 동시에 전적으로 새로운 창조의 날이다. 하루하루가 최초의 날이고 하루하루가 신생의 지평이다. 이 새로운 하루가 주는 인연에 감동하는 능력을 잃어버리고 감사하는 능력을 잃어버리고 감내하는 힘을 잃어버리면, 인생은 고통의 바다가 되고 만다. 그 우울과 불안과 허기를 채우기 위해 재미와 마취와 소유의 중독으로 하루하루 시들어갈 뿐이다.

갑갑하고 피로하고 단조로운 일상이 엄존할지라도, 이 지상에서 나의 하루하루는 내가 생각하는 것보다 훨씬 더 고귀하고 신비롭고 장엄한 것일 수 있음을 나는 강렬히 느낀다. 우리는 삶이라는 선물을 마음껏 누려야 한다. 나에게 주어진 하루하루를 남김없이 살아야 한다. 인생의 골수까지 맛보며 살아낸 시간, 여성의 놀라움과 불꽃의 만남의 시간, 눈부신 절정체험이 내면의 느낌으로 새겨지는 시간, 영원의 시간으로 합류하는 생의 시간, 그 '긴 하루'를 살아야 한다.

오늘 하루 얼마나 감동하며 깨달았는가. 얼마나 감사하며 나누었는가. 얼마나 감내하며 사랑했는가. 그리하여 오늘 하루 얼마나 더 나아진 내가 되었는가. 일도 사랑도 혁명도 그 모든 것의 목적은 지금 여기의 하루, 진정한 나로 살아있는 하루, 그토록 애써온 노고와 눈물로 걸어온 날들이 내적 성숙으로 익어 바쳐지는 생의 '하루'가 아니겠는가.

그러니 항상 노래를 부르기를. 먼저 미소를 짓기를. 귀를 크게 열어놓기를. 따뜻한 손으로 어루만지기를. 새로운 눈으로 아름답고 고귀한 것을 알아보기를. 탁 트인 호감으로 마주 걸어오는 인연의 신비를 맞이하기를. 곧고 선한 마음으로 불의 앞에 아니오! 거절하기를.

나는 이 모든 것을 나보다 먼저 죽은 동지들과 죽은 나의 어머니와 나보다 더 참혹하고 고독했던 선배 혁명가와 순교자들에게 배웠다. 그리고 나보다 더 가난하고 힘든 처지에서도 최선을 다해 살고 사랑하고, 서로 돕고 나누고, 나무를 심고 꽃을 피워내는 여기 사진 속 사람들에게 배웠다.

　이 필사적인 자기 홍보와 인정 투쟁의 시대에, 누가 보아주고 알
아주지 않아도 허리 숙여 심고 기르며 세상에 꼭 필요한 일을 해나가
는 사람들. 어떤 대가와 보상이 없어도 나직이 자신을 내어주는 헌신
의 사람들. 상상하기 힘든 고통과 시련 가운데서도 결코 자신에게 주
어진 하루를 함부로 살지 않는 사람들. 카메라를 든 내가 할 수 있고
해야 하는 일은 그 숨은 빛의 사람을 알아보고, 경외하고, 사랑하는 일
밖에 없으니. 나의 사진과 글은 평범한 사람들의 평범한 하루 속에 살
아있는 좋은 삶의 원형과 고귀한 인간성을 알아보고 그 '희망의 씨알'
을 그대 순정한 가슴에 전해주는 것이니.

　지금 여기, 지구 인류의 다양한 하루를 마주하며 우리가 잃어버린
것이 무엇인지, 진정 원하는 것이 무엇인지를 묵상하며 내 안에 이미
있는 빛나는 길을 찾아가기를 바라는 마음이다. 하루, 긴 하루, 나만의
다른 하루를.

　나는 하루 하루 살아왔다. 감동하고 감사하고 감내하며.

2019년 10월
박노해

Preface

A Long Day's Life

What a long day my childhood was.

Those were days when I woke to the sound of birdsong early in the morning, and my first task was to sweep up the red persimmon leaves and withered petals that had fallen onto the yard. When the sunlight shone onto the tidy yard with its neat broom marks, my mother who had been preparing breakfast would make me sit on the floor, smile, and say, 'You've worked hard. It looks pretty, doesn't it?' Then I would quickly follow my sister, who carried a water-pot on her head, to the spring and back, wash my face in cold water, and when it was time for me to go to school, above my head red dragonflies and sparrows would follow, teasing me as I walked along the path between the rice fields lined with tall millet and sunflowers. As I sat in the classroom, through the window I would watch white clouds float past, flocks of geese setting off on migration, and in the small library, as I read letters like little black seeds with dreams more famished than my famished stomach, I would forget time, immersed in adventures that made my heart beat fast. After exiting the school gate, I used to walk past the marketplace, explore here and there, then come home carrying asters and wild chrysanthemums I had picked. There I collected the warm eggs that the hens had laid and put them in a basket, looking forward to market day. I would take out the goat, leave it tethered on the grassy embankment, go running down to the sea with my playmates, and catch shad or mullet. Those I wrapped in reeds, took them home, quickly tossed them into the kitchen, and ran out again. What with cheering in support of older friends as they played volleyball for a dish of pumpkin porridge in the rice mill yard, then playing at horse-riding, engaging in one-legged fights, play at kickball and marbles, it was sunset before we realized. "Children, supper's ready, come and eat, you can play again tomorrow." At the sound of mothers calling from every alley, we all went back to our various homes, where the evening smoke was rising, to eat, then reluctantly doing our homework, writing our diaries, all the time licking our pencils, spent heart-aching evenings secretly writing and erasing letters to the girl I liked. Finally, I would lie on my mother's lap as she prayed the rosary beneath a kerosene lamp, doze off, then feel a need to pee, go out, gaze at the host of stars shining in the dark, go back indoors away from the chill breeze, snuggle under the bedding, and fall into a dead sleep.

Our days then were long days. Each day was full, despite poverty and misfortune. Those were days when we had no sweet, greasy food, no entertaining devices, no television, no smartphones, no computers, but the lack of them, combined with boredom, stimulated a human abundance, friendship, and interests, helped develop an ability to be independent, to live for others. Those were days when long-lasting hours filled with blank spaces and new impressions became an ample stage enabling us to live and move independently, giving birth to imagination, creativity, and storytelling, kindling a fervor for dizzying adventures and explorations, unknown to grown-ups. Such abundant poverty and such dazzling long days were alive for us.

Ah, but good times are not the only long days. Times of hurt and pain were also long days. When my country was challenged by division and dictatorship, my youth was also a long day when I was tormented with sorrow and anger, labored, read, organized, and struggled. Hours of war-like, all-night labor, hours of sorrowful, depressing contempt and discrimination, poignant hours of defeat and frustration of helpless love, hours of torture when I bled like a captive beast, hours of life imprisonment in a prison's solitary cell, trapped in a blue shroud, and hours when, though free, I passed through scenes of conflict full of tension and horror, desolate hours spent crossing deserts, plains, and plateaus amidst snow-peaked mountains. My life has truly been a long day, a day of days.

The years grow longer, the years grow shorter, the days remaining are less numerous than the days already past, and you come to realize after passing through the gates of life's few stages that for everyone, childhood passes by quickly like a child growing up, youth that was so splendid likewise passes by in a flash, yet even that cold-hearted time lives in me as nothing more than one long day; that amidst all those many days, only one long day remains, yearned for, a tearful memory, and that long day was a day when I was truly alive. Amidst vain lives passing in competing and speeding to own more, rise higher, surely that long day of days will be the fruit of this life given to each person. Even amidst constantly repeated everyday life, that long day will live and be the strength that makes me stand up again, pushes me in the back, makes me move ahead.

For the past twenty years I have been visiting the farthest, highest and deepest villages on earth. As a vagabond of the global age, I have visited villages that do not even figure on any map. Truly. From the beginning, the goal of my journeying was here. One day, one long day, another day.

'One day'. Truly 'one day' is a word that is ordinary and wonderful, commonplace and frightening. Because, just as one drop of water contains the whole sky, each day is a whole life, 一日一生, a day in which eternity dwells. But our today's day has become time sunk and enclosed in a material world separated from eternity and divinity. The present age is an age where you cannot live without money, and there is no life even if you have money. As a result, life always flows from one "preparation" to another "preparation," while life here and now has become a series of pain endured for the sake of the future. In human history, we hesitate to live the moment fully when our existence isn't guaranteed in the future. But we have no future. There can only be hope.

If I do not live my own day, something takes my day from me. If I do not study myself, someone studies me and uses me as a resource. Surely the ultimate goal that all the forces of evil seek to dominate, the last territory that the powers of globalized capital hope to occupy, is my inner self and my daily tasks. Thus our inner life and everyday life are silent battlefields. That is the front line of this age. Now, in my inner life and daily life, the mystery of evil and the leap of good are fighting each other. Good and evil, love and greed, beauty and baseness begin and end in my inner life and everyday life.

Tangled up in this civilization's radical monopoly system, even if I live every day acutely aware of my own helplessness, we cannot give up our struggle to find a true self, live a good life, and advance toward a better world. Even if we keep failing and growing frustrated, starting again and steadily pushing ahead is the ordinary day-by-day greatness that is given to me every day.

I know the weight of that day. It was when I fell victim to the military dictatorship and was dragged down to a secret chamber in the basement of the National Security Agency to be tortured. The days in that torture chamber, where 50 people took turns 24 hours a day, was a pure white time full of screaming where neither will, thought nor determination were of any use. What they asked for was simple: 'Name just one!' But if I were to name one comrade, they would push on to the bitter end: 'Just one more. One more!'

The order that enabled me to pass through that was just one phrase: 'Just one day more! One day more! I've survived this far, surely today's my end, the last day of my life. So just this one more day, today! One more day, until my last minute, and death!' And so, it seemed, 24 days passed.

Whether it be life or history, perhaps the most decisive term might be that phrase: 'Just one day more' versus 'just one more'. When a person compromises on 'just one more,' when that one breaks, one by one he surrenders the whole of himself. Thus my mission is just one day. Our hope, our love, and our revolution are each just one day. 'One more versus one day more'. So today again I walk along the path of my first heart, day by day.

Whenever I return to a modern city after going on foot to visit the most remote, highest global villages, where for centuries day has followed day, I experience a jetlag from distant life. This is an age where everyone knows everything and becomes smart at too high a speed and in a flood of information. I feel that the most important capability in life is being lost. That is the power to be touched, the power to be thankful, and the power to endure.

For any living person, today is both a recurring routine and an entirely new day of creation. Day by day is the first day, and day by day is the horizon of a new birth. If the ability to be touched by the human relationships offered by this new day is lost, the ability to be thankful is lost, and the strength to endure is lost, life becomes a sea of pain. Each day will only wither away, poisoned by the amusements, the anesthetics, and the possessions used to fill up the depression, the anxiety and the hunger.

Even though cramped, weary, monotonous daily life really exists, I feel intensely that my every day on earth can be far more noble, mysterious, and majestic than I think. We must enjoy the gift of life to the full. I have to live entirely every day given to me. Times spent savoring life to the marrow, times of journey's surprises and pyrotechnic encounters, times when intensely dazzling experiences make a deep impression on inner feelings, and times of life join with the time of eternity, such is the 'long day' I have to live.

How much have you been moved and enlightened today? How much have you been thankful for and shared? How much have you persevered and loved? How much a better person have I become today? Surely, whether it be work, love, or revolution, the purpose of them all, this day here and now, the day I am living as my true self, the days I have walked through with so much effort and tears, are all "one day" devoted to developing inner maturity.

So may I always sing. May I smile first. May I keep my ears wide open. May I touch with warm hands. May I recognize what is beautiful and noble with new eyes. May I welcome with open-eyed goodwill the mystery of meeting coming toward me. May I refuse injustice with a firm and good heart, saying 'No!'

I learned all of this from my comrades who died before me, my deceased mother, older revolutionaries and martyrs who suffered more and were more lonely than I. And I also learned it from all the people in these pictures who, though they are poorer and have harder lives than myself, live and love with all their might, help each other and share, plant trees and grow flowers.

In this age of desperate self-promotion and struggle for recognition, here are people who bend down, sow and nurture and do what is surely necessary for the world without anyone seeing or knowing. Dedicated people who devote themselves without compensation or reward. People who never live heedlessly the day given to them, even in the midst of pain and trials that are hard to imagine. All I can and must do with my camera is to recognize, venerate and love the people of hidden light. My photos and writings are intended to help recognize the true form of the good life and noble humanity found in the ordinary days of ordinary people, and convey a "seed of hope" to your pure heart.

Here and now, faced with the varied days of the people of the world, contemplating what we have lost and what we really want, I hope to find the shining path that already exists within me. One day, one long day, a day of my own.

I have lived day by day. I am touched, give thanks, endure.

October, 2019
Park Nohae

𝄇

여 명 에 물 을 긷 다

여명은 생의 신비다.

밤이 걸어오고 다시 태양이 밝아오면

오늘 하루 새로운 인생을 시작한다.

에티오피아 고원에서 하루의 시작은

먼 길을 걸어 물을 길어 오는 것.

이 물로 밥을 짓고 몸을 씻고 가축의 목을 축이리라.

짐을 진 발걸음은 무겁고 느리지만

이 삶의 무게에 사랑이 있고 희망이 있다면

기꺼이 그것을 감내할 힘이 생겨나느니.

나는 하루 하루 살아왔다.

감동하고 감사하고 감내하며.

2

DRAWING WATER AT DAYBREAK

Daybreak is life's mystery. When night comes walking then the sun rises again, a new life begins. As day dawns in the Ethiopian Highlands, I return home from a long journey to draw water. With this water, I will wash rice, wash myself, and quench the cattle's thirst. My steps bearing such a burden are heavy and slow but if there is love and hope in the weight of this life's burdens, the strength to endure is given. I have ever lived day by day. I am touched, give thanks, endure.

Lalibela, Ethiopia, 2009.

아 침 마 다 꽃

다친 아빠를 돌보다 엄마도 몸이 아프다.
이른 아침 산에 올라 땔나무를 해오는 어린 딸.
이슬 맺힌 연초록 아웅더비 꽃을 꺾어 들고 와
집안 불전에 바치며 하루를 시작한다.
버마에서는 아무리 가난한 집이라도
매일 아침 꽃을 사서 불전에 바친다.
사람은 밥이 없이는 살 수 없지만
영혼이 없는 밥은, 경외가 없는 삶은,
시든 꽃잎처럼 사라지고 마는 덧없는 생이기에.

2

EVERY MORNING FLOWERS

Her mother is sick from looking after her injured father. Early each morning, their young daughter climbs the hills to gather firewood. She returns bringing dew-covered green Aung Thabyae flowers and begins the day by offering them at the household Buddha shrine. In Burma, no matter how poor a family may be, every morning they buy flowers and offer them at the Buddha shrine. No one can live without rice but rice without a soul, life without awe is a fleeting life that disappears like a dead petal.

Palaung village, Kalaw, Burma, 2011.

SUNLIGHT IN A TEACUP

The daily routine in high mountain villages starts before sunrise. As day dawns, they draw water, pick greens, feed the cattle and sweep the garden, what has to be done today is done quickly. Finally, as the sun rises, they wash themselves and prepare tea. In the morning fish dry savory in the smoke from the fire and the family pass round cups of tea and chatter. The life that comes shaking off darkness teaches. As we open our eyes each morning, we see a world dazzling in sunshine. What a wonder that another day has been given to me! What a great blessing it is to drink tea infused with sunshine and see each other's smiling faces!

Palaung village, Kalaw, Burma, 2011.

찻잔에 햇살을 담아

높은 산마을의 일과는 '해 뜨기 전에'이다.
여명 속에서 물을 긷고 나물을 따고 가축을 먹이고
마당을 쓸고 오늘 할 일을 훌쩍 해내버린다.
이윽고 태양이 떠오르면 몸을 씻고 차를 끓인다.
모닥불 연기에 물고기가 고소하게 말라가고,
식구들끼리 찻잔을 건네며 담소를 나누는 아침.
어둠 속을 떨며 걸어온 인생은 알리라.
아침에 눈을 뜨면 햇살에 눈부신 세상이 있고
나에게 또 하루가 주어졌다는 게 얼마나 큰 경이인지.
햇살을 담은 차를 마시며 서로의 웃는 얼굴을
바라볼 수 있다는 게 얼마나 큰 축복인지.

카르툼 새벽 시장

청나일강과 백나일강이 만나는 사막에
저 유명한 카르툼 새벽 시장이 열린다.
이렇게 풍성하고 다양하고 정갈하고
원색의 생명력이 출렁이는 장이 또 있을까.
직접 기른 양파를 정성껏 쌓아놓은 상인이
여럿이 돌려보는 귀한 신문을 펼쳐 읽는다.
먹고 사는 게 우선이지만 내가 사는 세계가
어떻게 돌아가는지 알아야 하지 않겠냐고
아침 눈빛으로 세상을 읽어 나간다.

2

DAWN MARKET IN KHARTOUM

In the desert where the Blue Nile and the White Nile meet the celebrated Khartoum dawn market is being held. Is there any other market as vibrant with such rich, varied, tidy, vivid vitality? After carefully stacking onions he has grown, a merchant opens and reads a precious newspaper that many read in turns. Eating and living are the first priority, of course, but I need to know how the world I live in is going. He reads about the world with bright morning eyes.

Khartoum, Sudan, 2008.

AN OLD TEAK WOOD BRIDGE

The longest and oldest wooden bridge in the world. Standing with its firm frame though all kinds of storms, it supports today with its long centuries of being. The wooden bridge I crossed in the morning sunlight I can cross again at evening twilight, but I can never pass a second time through the time I spent today. So it is said that we have to live eternity today, seeming to refer to U-Bein Bridge in Mandalay at dawn.

Lake Taungthaman, Mandalay, Burma, 2011.

오 래 된 티 크 나 무 다 리

세계에서 가장 길고 오래된 목조 다리.
온갖 풍랑에도 곧은 뼈대로 버티고 선 채
수백 년의 세월로 오늘을 받쳐주고 있다.
아침 햇살에 건너간 나무 다리는
저녁노을에 다시 건너올 수 있지만
오늘 건너간 하루는 다시 돌아올 수 없다.
그러니 하루 속에 영원을 살아가야 한다고
동틀 녘의 우삐인 다리가 말하는 것만 같다.

인 레 호 수 의 고 기 잡 이

'버마의 심장'이라 불리는 인레 호수는
고원 지대에 지리한 '산 위의 바다'이다.
희푸름한 물안개 속에 햇살이 빛나면
인레 어부들은 가만가만 외발로 노를 저어간다.
"리듬에 맞춰야 해요. 고유한 리듬에 맞춰야 해요."
그물을 당겨 은빛 물고기를 거두어 받는 시간,
청년의 노동은 우아한 춤이 된다.

₹

FISHING IN INLE LAKE

Inle Lake, known as 'the heart of Burma,' is a 'sea in the mountains,' located
in the highlands. When the sun shines through the blue mist, the Inle
fishermen gently row with a single foot. "I have to keep the rhythm. I have to
keep the unique rhythm." When it's time to draw up the nets and harvest the
silvery fish, youth's work becomes a stately dance.

Lake Inle, Nyaung Shwe, Burma, 2011.

씨 앗 을 심 는 사 람

세계에서 화산이 가장 많은 땅 인도네시아.

혁명의 날이 그러하듯 화산 폭발은

두려움과 동시에 비옥한 대지를 선물한다.

아침 안개 속에 씨감자를 심어가는 라당의 농부들.

살아있는 인간은 날마다 무언가를 심고 씨 뿌려간다.

말의 씨앗인 말씨로도, 마음의 씨앗인 마음씨로도

세상 깊은 곳에 좋고 나쁜 씨앗을 심어간다.

2

THE SOWER OF SEEDS

Indonesia has the largest number of volcanoes in the world. Like days of revolution, volcanic eruptions bring gifts both of fear and fertile ground. Farmers in Ladang plant seed potatoes in the morning mist. Living human beings plant, sow seeds every day. They plant good and bad seeds deep in the world, the seeds of words, the seeds of hearts.

Ngadas village, Malang, East Java, Indonesia, 2013.

목 화 송 이 를 따 는 소 녀

인더스 문명이 탄생한 땅, 파키스탄과 인디아에서
전 세계 목화솜의 3분의 1 이상이 생산된다.
날카로운 꽃받침에 감싸인 목화솜을 하나하나
골라 따내는 소녀들의 손에는 핏방울이 붉은데
그 손으로 따낸 목화솜은 눈이 부시게 희어서
면 옷을 입고 쓰는 나는 불현듯 심장을 찔린다.

ℛ

GIRLS PICKING COTTON

In the lands where the Indus civilization was born, Pakistan and India, more
than one-third of the world's cotton is produced. As they pick the cotton
bolls, each enclosed in a prickly calyx, drops of red blood dye the hands of the
girls and the cotton bolls they pick with those hands are so dazzlingly white
that I who wear cotton clothes am suddenly stabbed to the heart.

Bahawalpur, Punjab, Pakistan, 2011.

갠지스강의 여인들

갠지스강가의 공사에 나선 일용직 여성들이
무거운 돌을 이고 불볕의 대지를 걷는다.
지상의 어떤 기둥보다 더 강인한 살아 움직이는
기둥이 되어 세상을 떠받치고 있는 것만 같다.
가난 속에서도 내면의 빛과 기품을 잃지 않겠다는 듯
빨강 파랑 노랑 하늘빛 사리를 날리며 느릿느릿
곧고 치열한 걸음으로 차별의 세상을 걸어나간다.

❧

WOMEN BY THE GANGES RIVER

Women out repairing the banks of the Ganges as day-workers carry heavy stones, walk on earth scorched by the burning sun. Becoming living, moving pillars, stronger than any pillar on earth, they seem to be pillars supporting the world. Determined not to lose their inner light and grace in poverty, dressed in red, blue, yellow, azure saris, erect, they slowly walk with resolute steps through a world of discrimination.

Varanasi, Uttar Pradesh, India, 2013.

BARLEY HARVEST ON THE
TIBETAN PLATEAU

After China occupied Tibet, it forced the Tibetans to plant wheat and rice instead of their traditional barley. They did not fit the climate and the crops failed, numerous people died of famine. So Tibetans started planting barley again. "Tsampa made of barley is our souls' food. We have to eat tsampa in order to be Tibetan." Still now their land, their days do not belong to them, but still the sound of Tibetan women laughing and singing, a sound that cannot be conquered with guns and swords, makes the barley fields sway.

Amuquhu village, Shankar, Amdo Tibet, 2012.

티 베 트 고 원 의 보 리 수 확

중국은 티베트를 점령한 후 티베트인들의
전통 작물인 보리 대신 밀과 쌀을 심게 했다.
기후와 풍토에 맞지 않아 흉작이 이어졌고
수많은 사람이 기근으로 죽어갔다.
다시 보리를 심기 시작한 티베트인들.
"보리로 만든 짬빠는 우리 영혼의 양식이지요.
짬빠를 먹어야 티베트인이지요."
지금도 빼앗긴 땅, 빼앗긴 날이지만
총칼로도 빼앗지 못할 티베트 여인들의
웃음소리 노랫소리가 보리밭을 흔든다.

볼리비아 광부들의 퇴근길

세계의 주요 주석 생산국인 볼리비아 최대 광산 우아누니.
1952년 부패한 정부와 기업에 맞서 광부들이 주도한
'볼리비아 혁명'으로 국영화된 광산이다.
당시 혁명에 나선 광부들은 군부독재를 뒤엎고
원주민의 선거권과 토지개혁까지 쟁취해냈다.
혁명의 기억을 이어온 광부들은 오늘도 민중의 전위로
사회 개혁을 밀어가며 저항과 용기의 원천이 되고 있다.

2

BOLIVIAN MINERS RETURNING HOME

Bolivia, the main producer of tin in the world, with its largest mine, Huanuni.
In 1952, it was nationalized in the "Bolivian Revolution" led by the miners
against corrupt government and corporations. The miners who led the
revolution overturned the military dictatorship, won the right to vote for
indigenous people and even obtained land reform. The miners today, keeping
alive the memory of the revolution, lead the way as part of the people in
pushing for social reforms, becoming a source of resistance and courage.

Huanuni, Oruro, Bolivia, 2010.

눈부신 지상의 시간

새벽부터 캄캄한 지하 갱도에서 일한 광부가

푸른 하늘을 바라보며 눈을 가늘게 뜬다.

"지상은 내게 늘 눈이 부셔 눈물이 나요.

오늘도 세상은 해가 떴구나.

오늘도 내가 살아 나왔구나.

열두 살 때부터 광부로 일을 했어요.

어른들이 못 들어가는 좁은 갱도를 개척했지요.

지상에서 산 날보다 지하의 날들이 더 많았네요.

세상이 조금은 더 환해진 거겠죠.

지상의 환한 햇살만 보면… 그냥 눈물이 나요."

2

DAZZLING TIME ABOVE GROUND

A miner who has worked in a dark underground tunnel since dawn gazes up at the blue sky and squints his eyes. "Here above ground it's always so dazzling it makes me cry. Look, the sun rose on the world again today! I have come up alive again today! I have been working as a miner since I was 12 years old. I used to work in narrow tunnels that adults could not enter. I have spent more days underground than above ground. The world has maybe grown a bit brighter. When I see the sunshine above ground… I just cry."

Huanuni, Oruro, Bolivia, 2010.

당당한 귀항

인도양 푸른 파도가 철썩이는 베따꾼 어촌.
붉은 석양을 받으며 먼바다로 떠난 어부들이
밤새 파도와 싸우며 잡은 물고기를 싣고 귀항한다.
배가 없는 가난한 이들은 일을 거든 후 일용할 물고기를
조금씩 나눠 받으며 만선의 기쁨을 함께한다.
어깨에 짊어진 묵직한 물고기를 팔아서
막내 아이 교복을 사 입힐 생각에 흐뭇한 어부는
파도 속 격한 노동의 피로가 달콤하기만 하다.

2

A DIGNIFIED RETURN

Betakkun is a fishing village pounded by the blue waves of the Indian
Ocean. Fishermen who set off for far away with the red sunset, bring home
their catch after fighting with the waves all night long. Poor folk who have
no boat help out then receive some fish in return, sharing with all the joy
of a full load of fish. After selling the heavy fish borne on his shoulders,
a fisherman is delighted to think he can buy his youngest child a school
uniform. The fatigue from laboring in the waves is so sweet.

Puri, Orissa, India, 2013.

HARVESTING POTATOES ON THE
ANDES PLATEAU

This is a day for harvesting potatoes by the village's combined labor on the
Andes Plateau, birthplace of humanity's potatoes. The owner of the field
whose turn it is today is grateful. We of necessity need each other, so he
thanks all who thus share their strength. Glad to see all the faces gathered
together, he keeps handing round cups of Chicha corn liquor. As the icy wind
from snowy peaks dries their sweat, the sound of young men and women
singing, talking and laughing is never-ending. The first potatoes, grown in
the Andes 8,000 years ago, every time the world's potatoes fall sick and are
in crisis, are shared out again, as the last remaining 'seeds of hope.' Even if
today's world is swept away, shipwrecked, loses its way, the 'seeds of hope'
live on in this lofty place, and so long as the leading young folk who guard
them remain alive, 'our day' is not yet over.

Maras, Cusco, Peru, 2010.

안데스 고원의 감자 수확

인류의 '감자 종갓집' 안데스 고원에서
마을 두레노동으로 감자 수확을 하는 날.
오늘 순번인 밭 주인은 그저 고맙다고
우리가 서로를 필요로 할 수밖에 없고
서로의 힘을 나눌 수 있어 고맙다고
이렇게 모여서 얼굴만 봐도 좋다고
연신 옥수수 막걸리 치차를 돌린다.
만년설산 시린 바람에 땀방울을 씻으며,
젊은 남녀의 노랫소리 이야기 소리
풋풋한 웃음소리가 끊이지 않는다.
8천 년 전 안데스에서 최초로 재배된 감자는
세계의 감자가 병들어 위기에 처할 때마다
마지막 남은 '희망의 씨알'처럼 나누어졌다.
오늘 세계가 난파선처럼 휩쓸리며 앞을 잃어도
저 높은 곳의 '희망의 씨알'이 살아있고
그것을 지켜가는 '젊은 전위들'이 살아있다면,
그러면, 아직 '우리의 하루'는 끝나지 않았다.

흙 지 붕 마 당 의 담 소

만년설산에 둘러싸인 파슈툰 마을.
오전 노동을 마치고 흙지붕 마당에 모여
빵과 차를 나누는 느긋한 시간이다.
어른들은 아이와 청년이 있어
말을 삼가며 위엄을 지키고
아이들은 예의를 갖추며 지혜를 배운다.
"우리의 계율은 우애와 환대이지요.
삶의 마당에 우정과 사귐의 꽃을 피우고
이방인을 반기며 빵과 차를 나누는 거죠.
차를 마시는 시간이 없는 하루는
아무리 부유해도 메마른 하루이지요.
친구가 찾아오지 않는 집안은
아무리 부귀해도 가난한 집안이지요."

2

TALKING IN AN EARTH-ROOFED YARD

A Pashtun village surrounded by snow-covered mountains. After the
morning labor is done, gathered in the earth-roofed yard, a relaxing moment
sharing bread and tea. Since children and young people are present, the
adults are guarded in speech, keep their dignity. The children are polite,
learn wisdom. "Our rule is friendship and hospitality. In the yard of life,
flowers of friendship and fellowship blossom as we welcome strangers, share
bread and tea. Even one day without drinking tea, no matter how prosperous
you may be, is a thirsty day. A household where no friend comes visiting, no
matter how rich, is a poor family."

Drosh, Khyber Pakhtunkhwa, Pakistan, 2011.

OFF WE GO, YAKS, BACK TO
OUR HOME ON THE GRASSLANDS

Nomadic Tibetans with their herds of yaks. This lofty, vast grasslands is brimming with blue skies, clear winds, wild flowers, night's darkness and calm, with freedom, freedom. The only thing missing is people. "Off we go, yaks. Let's go home. You've filled your stomachs with green grass, now I need satisfy my hunger, too. I have to go back to my dear ger where my wife has cooked supper and is waiting for me. Off we go, yaks, back to our home on the grasslands."

Shankar, Amdo Tibet, 2012.

가자 야크들아, 초원의 집으로

야크 떼를 몰고 유랑하는 티베트인들.
이 높고 넓은 초원에 넘치는 건
푸른 하늘과 맑은 바람과 야생들꽃,
밤의 어둠과 고요 그리고 자유, 자유다.
단 하나 그리운 건 사람이다.
"가자, 야크들아. 집으로 돌아가자.
너는 푸른 풀로 배를 채웠으니
이제 나의 고픔을 채워야겠다.
내 사람이 밥을 지어 기다리는
그리운 게르로 돌아가야겠다.
가자 야크들아, 초원의 집으로 돌아가자."

네 아이의 엄마

고산지대 소수민족이 사는 동향족 마을.
감자 농사를 짓던 엄마가 잠시 집으로 돌아와
아가에게 젖을 먹이고 낮잠을 재운다.
"이 아이가 넷째인데 딸을 한 명 더 낳고 싶어요.
아이들은 형제자매가 많을수록 잘 자라거든요.
다투기도 하고 화해도 하면서 서로 돌봐주니까요.
의지할 존재가 있는 것만큼 듬직한 건 없으니까요.
아이들은 제가 젖만 물려주면 스스로 자라나요.
태어날 때 자기 먹을 건 다 갖고 태어난다잖아요."

R

A MOTHER OF FOUR

In Dong Xiang, the village of an ethnic minority high in the mountains, a mother, who has been harvesting potatoes, goes home, gives her baby the breast, dozes briefly. "This is our fourth child and I want to have one more daughter. The more siblings children have, the better they grow up, because they take care of each other, squabbling and reconciling. Nothing is more important than having someone you can lean on. I just breast feed the children and they grow up all by themselves. It's said that when you're born, you're born with everything you will ever eat."

Dongxiangxian, Gansusheng, China, 2012.

형 제 이 발 소

이웃 마을 여자친구를 만나러 가는 형을 위해
솜씨 좋은 남동생이 멋지게 머리를 깎아준다.
"우리 형은요, 진짜 일솜씨 끝내주고
말썽쟁이 친구들 다 챙겨주고
노래도 잘하고 생선 요리는 동네 최고예요.
딱 하나, 말수가 적고 여자 앞에서 수줍어요.
남자들이 진짜 여자는 몰라보고 외모에 홀리듯
여자애들도 속 깊은 남자를 몰라본다니까요.
실은 형이 빨리 장가를 가야 저도 쫌⋯ 하하하."

2

BROTHER'S BARBERSHOP

Before his older brother goes to meet his girlfriend in a nearby village his
skillful younger brother cuts his hair neatly. "My older brother's skill at work
is awesome. He takes care of all his mischievous friends, he sings well and
he's the best at cooking fish in all the neighborhood. Only one problem, he's
a man of few words, and shy in front of girls. Just as men don't appreciate real
women, are only bewitched by their looks, so too women fail to appreciate
a man who's deep inside. Actually, I hope he gets married soon, then it's my
turn… Hahaha."

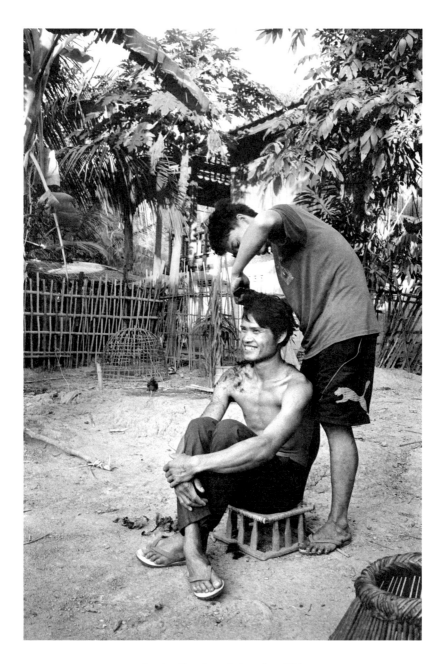

Songcha village, Luang Prabang, Laos, 2011.

THE TRUE EDUCATION OF
'THE PLAYING TEACHER'

The wind that has passed over snowy peaks is icy, yet in the bright sunshine, apples ripen red and the young female teacher, a rare sight here, takes the children out for an outdoor class. "Now the sun and the wind are at their best. On such days, study should be short, and playing long. I want the children to enjoy the blessings of the season fully. We cannot give up today for the sake of the future. Surely life means living every day fully. So they call me 'the playing teacher.' Ho Ho."

Nasirabad village, Northern Areas, Pakistan, 2011.

'날 라 리 선 생'의 참 교 육

만년설산을 지나온 바람은 시리지만
맑은 햇살에 사과알은 빨갛게 익어가고,
이곳에 정말 드문 젊은 여선생님은
아이들을 데리고 나와 야외 수업을 한다.
"지금이 햇살과 바람이 젤 좋을 때니까요.
이런 날은 공부는 짧게, 노는 건 길게.
아이들이 계절의 축복을 마음껏 누렸으면 해요.
미래를 위한다고 오늘을 포기할 순 없잖아요.
하루하루 제때제때 다 살아야 삶이 아닌가요.
그래서 저를 '날라리 선생'이라 부른대요. 호호."

맨 발 의 메 시 처 럼

이곳 소년들에게 축구가 없는 하루는 없다.
대나무를 잘라다 폐타이어로 이어 박아
직접 골대를 만들어 세운 아이들.
맨발의 메시처럼 패스하고 슛을 날린다.
아이들은 대지에서 자유롭게 뛰놀기만 하면
자기 안의 푸른 야생의 생명력이 깨어난다.
아이들에게 더 많은 자연을,
더 많은 모험과 더 많은 신비를.

☙

LIKE A BAREFOOTED MESSI

For boys around here, no day passes without soccer. Cutting bamboos, joining
them with old tires and planting them in the ground, children make their own
goalposts, then pass and shoot like barefooted Messi. Once children can run
and play freely on the ground, a wild green life awakes inside them. Give the
children more nature, more adventure and more mystery.

Sukamukti, Sukabumi, West Java, Indonesia, 2013.

물 소 와 함 께 물 장 구

한낮의 더운 노동에 지친 물소를 씻겨주려
강으로 할아버지를 따라나선 아이들.
물소와 함께 강물에 뛰어들어 물장구를 친다.
새끼 때부터 함께 자란 물소는 시원한 강물과
아이들의 장난에 기분 좋은 울음소리를 낸다.
행여 거센 물살에 휩쓸리는 아이들을 구해내는
든든한 지킴이도 물소이다.

2

SPLASHING ABOUT WITH
WATER BUFFALO

Children follow their grandfather to the river to wash the water buffalo
that's weary from working in the heat of the day. They jump into the river
with the water buffalo and splash about. The water buffalo, that grew up
with the children since it was small, lows happily at the children's playfulness
and the cool river. The water buffalo is also a strong guard, ready to rescue
any children who are swept away by the fierce current.

In Dein, Nyaung Shwe, Burma, 2011.

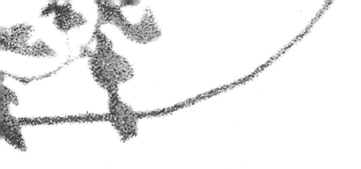

A GIRL GROWING TREES

In a remote Fakheer village where desolate landscapes unfold, when desertification dried the rivers, dried the earth and the trees died, the villagers gradually moved away to become urban laborers. In order to save the village, poor people decided to take a common reed, weave baskets, sell them, and plant trees. As the sun is setting, it is a daily ritual for a girl to give water to a young tree planted in the parched ground. "The day I was born my father planted an oak, saying: When you are 20 years old, we can sit in its shade and read a book. After 100 years, it will become a beautiful tree. After 300 years, it will be a green forest. So I have to cultivate it well for the future generations." Precious things ever require much time and effort. Our life is to plant green trees, breathing long.

Dohak Baba Fakheer village, Punjab, Pakistan, 2011.

나무를 키우는 소녀

황량한 풍경이 끝없이 펼쳐지는 파키르 오지 마을.
사막화로 강물이 마르고 땅이 마르고 나무가 죽어가자
하나둘 마을 사람들도 도시 노동자로 떠나갔다.
마을을 살리기 위해 가난한 주민들은
흔하게 널린 갈대를 엮어 만든
바구니를 팔아 나무를 심어 가기로 했다.
해가 기울 녘, 불볕의 땅에 심겨진 어린나무에
물을 길어다 주는 건 소녀의 하루 의례다.
"내가 태어나던 날 아빠는 오크 나무를 심었어요.
스무 살이 되면 나무그늘에 앉아 책을 읽자고.
100년이 지나면 아름드리 나무가 되고
300년이 흐르면 푸른 숲을 이룰 거라고.
그러니 대를 이어 가꿔가도록 잘 일러야 한다구요."
소중한 것들은 그만큼의 시간과 공력을 필요로 하는 법.
우리 삶은 긴 호흡으로 푸른 나무를 심어가는 것.

사 막 을 건 너 장 터 로 가 는 길

여인들이 땔감과 양 떼를 팔러 사막을 건너간다.
"어미가 낳을 때부터 직접 키운 양들이에요.
이 점박이 녀석은 겁이 많고요,
요 흰둥이는 울음소리가 크지요.
이제 다른 주인에게 보내려니 서운하고 슬프네요."
양들도 그 마음을 아는지 고개 숙여 걷는다.
하지만 오늘 번 돈으로 흙집도 늘리고 햇밀도 사고
아이를 학교에 보내리라는 소박한 희망으로
막막한 사막을 건너는 여인의 등허리가 곧다.

❧

THE ROAD ACROSS THE DESERT
TO THE MARKETPLACE

Women cross the desert to sell firewood and sheep. "These are sheep I've raised since their mothers gave birth. This speckled one is very timid, that white one bleats loudly. Now I feel sad because they're being sent to another owner." The sheep seem to know how she feels, walking with heads bent low. However, with the simple hope that they can use the money earned today to expand their clay house, buy fresh wheat, even send the children to school, the women crossing the boundless desert walk with straight backs.

Naga, Nubian, Sudan, 2008.

고산족 여인들의 작품

라오스 고산족의 작은 장이 열리는 날.
새벽부터 험한 산길을 걸어온 여인들이
깨끗하고 빳빳한 흰 보자기 위에다
직접 만든 싸리 빗자루, 새알만 한 감자알,
다듬은 줄콩들을 정성스레 펼쳐 놓는다.
세상의 숫자로는 몇 푼 안되는 초라한 것일지라도
숫자로는 매길 수 없는
그녀들의 인생과 노동의 작품이
단정히 빛나며 손님을 기다린다.

❧

THE WORK OF HILL-TRIBE WOMEN

A small market for hill-tribe villagers in Laos is open. On clean, stiff, white cloths the women, who have walked along steep mountain roads since dawn, carefully lay brooms they have made with twigs, potatoes the size of birds' eggs, long green beans. Even if they're poor things, worth just a few pence by the world's reckoning, those products of the women's life and labor, to which no price can be given in figures, shine neatly as they wait for customers.

Ban Phapoun Mai, Phongsali, Laos, 2011.

재 래 시 장 의 생 기

반다아체의 타케곤 재래시장.
햇밀을 빻아 뽑아낸 면발을 기름에 볶아
야생 버섯과 야채와 토종닭 육수에
뜨끈히 말아주는 국수 맛이 일품이다.
재래시장에는 삶의 생기가 맥박친다.
하루가 담긴 노동의 결실을 나누고
새로운 것들과 세상 소식이 흐르고
식구들의 먹을거리를 구하는 기쁨으로.

☙

VIGOR IN A TRADITIONAL MARKET

Takengon traditional market in Banda Aceh. Noodles made with fresh
wheat, fried in oil, with wild mushrooms, vegetables and chicken broth.
The taste of the piping hot noodles is the best. In a traditional market, life's
vigor pulsates. Sharing the fruits of each day's labor, new things and the
world's news flow by with the joy of buying food for the family.

Takengon, Central Aceh, Sumatra, Indonesia, 2013.

께로족 마을 총회

안데스 고원의 해발 5천 미터 께로족 마을 총회.
일곱 개 마을의 께로스인 전체가 한자리에 모여
공동의 대소사를 결정하는 여기가 이들의 국회다.
130여 명의 남녀노소가 초원에 둥글게 둘러앉아
전원합의에 도달할 때까지 서로 발언하고 경청한다.
공동체를 위한 시간은 빼놓을 수 없는 하루 일과다.
그 결정들이 내 삶의 하루를 변화시키기에.

✿

Q'ERO VILLAGE GENERAL ASSEMBLY

5,000 meters up on the Andes Plateau, the Q'ero village's General Assembly.
All the Q'ero people from seven villages are gathered together. These are
the parliaments that decide community affairs. 130 men and women, young
and old, sit in a circle on the grass, speak and listen to each other until a
unanimous agreement is reached. Time for the community is an indispensable
part of the day. And their decisions change the course of my daily life.

Cochamuco, Cusco, Peru, 2010.

'READING WHILE WALKING' IN THE WILDERNESS

A remote wilderness path infested with wolves and wild dogs. A child walking along after borrowing a book from the school library forgets time, forgets fear, as he reads while walking. A book is a long letter from a far-away friend and that letter offers secret adventures leading to other worlds, blazing encounters beyond time and space. So, seeming to sense that true reading is more thrilling than the wilderness beasts, the child is silently traversing the world bearing an inner fire.

Dohak Baba Fakheer village, Punjab, Pakistan, 2011.

황야의 '걷는 독서'

늑대와 승냥이가 출몰하는 황야의 오지길.
멀고 먼 길을 걸어 학교 도서관에서
한 권의 책을 빌려오는 아이는
시간도 잊고 무서움도 잊고 '걷는 독서' 중이다.
책이란 먼 데서 친구가 보내온 두꺼운 편지,
그 편지를 따라 다른 세계로 빠져들어 가는
비밀한 모험이자 시공을 넘어선 '불꽃의 만남'.
그리하여 참된 독서란 황야의 야수보다
더 아스라한 전율임을 아는 듯 아이는
내면의 불을 들고 고요히 세상을 횡단하고 있다.

하루 일을 마치는 인사

중국의 급격한 경제 개발로
티베트에도 경운기와 트랙터가 보급됐지만
많은 티베트인은 여전히 말이 끄는 쟁기를 쓴다.
농력 기계를 쓰면 땅이 굳을 뿐 아니라 빚을 지게 되고
무엇보다 오랜 세월 식구처럼 동행해온 말이 있기에.
종일 땅을 쟁기질한 농부가 가만히 말을 안아준다.
"이 하루도 고생 많았네. 우리 서로 수고했네.
자네가 없이는 나도 오늘 일을 못 했을 것이네.
오늘도 장하고 고맙네."
고단한 말도 슬며시 주인에게 기댄다.

❧

GREETINGS AFTER FINISHING
THE DAY'S WORK

With China's rapid economic development cultivators and tractors have been
introduced into Tibet, too, but still many Tibetans use horse-drawn plows.
Power machines not only harden the soil, they also create debts, and above
all, there is a horse that has accompanied me like family for many years.
A farmer, after plowing the ground all day, quietly hugs his horse: "You've
worked hard today. We worked hard together. Without you, I could not have
worked today. Thank you very much, you've been great today." As the weary
horse leans in silence on its master.

Labrang, Amdo Tibet, 2012.

고 요 속 의 묵 상

하루의 마무리는 고요 속의 묵상.
오래된 암벽 성전을 찾은 그녀가
홀로 깊은숨을 고르며 침잠하고 있다.
어디에서도 회의가 구름처럼 일어날 때
책상에 앉아서도 불안이 서성거릴 때
사람들 속에서 나를 잃는 것만 같을 때,
내 마음의 가장 깊은 곳에 가 닿는
침묵과 고독의 처소를 찾아갈 일이다.
고요히 차오르는 힘을 길어 올릴 일이다.

ၶ

MEDITATION IN SILENCE

Meditation in silence at the end of the day. A woman visits a shrine on a rock, stays silent alone, breathes deeply. When doubts arise like clouds, no matter where I am, when I feel anxious as I sit at my desk, when I feel I'm losing myself among people, I go to visit the deepest part of my heart, the place of silence and solitude, silently drawing up the strength rising there.

Lalibela, Ethiopia, 2008.

WHEN FATHER COMES HOME

Last night their father went down into the underground shafts of the Huanuni mine in Bolivia, carrying a full load of dynamite, and now his daughters rush to the mine entrance to greet him. His daughters cling to their father's arms, twittering like little birds. "Thanks to you, today again I emerge unscathed. Because my daughters are my guardian angels. Ha ha ha. I pray when I go down into the mine every day. So long as my children live their lives safely and the gifts they were born with blossom, that's fine. I always just smile once and go down into the mine." In this cruel world, completely devoted to one another, a smile that looks intently at faces, listens quietly, a smile drawn up with self-devotion, known as love, love, in painful, uneasy darkness.

Huanuni, Oruro, Bolivia, 2010.

아빠가 돌아올 때

볼리비아 우아누니 광산의 지하 갱도 속으로
어젯밤 다이너마이트를 가득 지고 들어간 아빠.
딸들은 광산 입구까지 달려가 아빠를 맞이한다.
작은 새처럼 지저귀며 아빠의 팔에 매달리는 딸들.
"오늘도 덕분에 무탈했네요.
딸들이 제 수호천사라서요. 하하하.
매일 광산으로 갈 때마다 기도하죠.
우리 아이들이 안전하게 자기 인생을 살고
타고난 걸 다 꽃피울 수 있다면, 네 그거죠.
나는 늘 한번 웃고 지하 막장으로 들어가죠."
이 무정한 세계에서 서로에게 온 존재를 기울여
가만가만 들어주고 얼굴을 바라봐주는 웃음.
괴롭고 불안한 어둠 속에서 사랑, 사랑이라는
자기 헌신으로 길어 올린 웃음.

흐르는 강물에 몸을 담고

버마의 태양은 사람을 달군다.

하지만 태양과 싸우지 말 일이다.

어디나 시원한 강물이 기다리고 있으니.

버마의 숲속 '강물 목욕탕'은 공짜다.

흐르는 강물에 몸을 담그기만 해도

하루의 근심과 피로가 씻겨 나가고

동그란 파문이 미소처럼 퍼져나간다.

❧

DIVING INTO A FLOWING RIVER

Burma's sun makes people hot. But you should not try to fight the sun. For cool rivers await you everywhere. Burma's forests' 'river bathhouse' is free. Just dive into a flowing river and all the day's worries and fatigue are washed away, as round ripples spread like smiles.

In Dein, Nyaung Shwe, Burma, 2011.

WASHING CLOTHES IN THE
IRRAWADDY RIVER

Originating from the Himalayas and running through Burma, the Irrawaddy River is the largest river in Burma. People build tiny huts near the river and live by their daily labor. "When I wash my clothes in the river, everything becomes clear. At present I have no land, no house, but I have a healthy body that can still work tomorrow, while the children are well-behaved and growing up strongly, so I keep looking ahead as I live."

River Irrawaddy, Mandalay, Burma, 2011.

이 라 와 디 강 가 의 빨 래

히말라야에서 발원해 버마를 종단하는
이라와디강은 버마 최대의 강이다.
강가 근처에 한 평짜리 움막을 짓고
일용직 노동으로 살아가는 사람들.
"강물에 빨래를 하다 보면 다 맑아져요.
지금은 땅도 없고 집도 없지만
내일도 일할 수 있는 성한 몸이 있고
아이들은 착하고 강하게 크고 있으니
앞을 바라보고 사는 거지요."

A RAJASTHAN WOMAN AT SUNSET

At sunset, when the blazing sun is growing gentle, a Rajasthan woman who
has finished her day's work washes her body and brings in the saris. "It's sad,
looking at the setting sun, somehow. Yet it's not setting, it's on its way back."
There is nothing sad about the end of a day. One who has lived a day fully, after
a sleep deeper than death is filled with new strength to face the new day.

Jaipur, Rajasthan, India, 2013.

석 양 빛 의 라 자 스 탄 여 인

불타오르던 태양이 순해지는 석양 녘.

하루 일을 마친 라자스탄 여인이

몸을 씻고 사리를 거두어들인다.

"지는 태양을 바라보는 건 왠지 슬퍼요.

그래도 지는 게 아니고 돌아오는 거니까요."

지는 하루를 슬퍼하지 말 일이다.

하루를 남김없이 살아낸 자는

죽음보다 깊은 단잠을 자고 나면

새로운 하루를 살아갈 새 힘이 차오르니.

지상의 저녁 밥상

노을이 물들어가면 지구마을의 골목마다
지상에서 가장 아름다운 노래가 울려온다.
"애야, 밥 먹고 내일 또 놀으렴."
엄마가 둥근 솥에서 피워내는 고소한 냄새에
아이들은 부엌까지 들어와 눈을 뗄 줄 모른다.
식사보다 더 신비로운 일상의 의식이 있을까.
죽은 것이 산 몸으로 화化하는 생명의 일치이고
하루하루 사랑과 신뢰로 이루어지는
영원한 삶의 잔치가 아닌가.

♫

SUPPER TABLE ON EARTH

When the glow of sunset begins to spread, in every alley of the global village the most beautiful song on earth rings out. "Children, let's eat, you can play again tomorrow." The smell that their mother produces from the round pot draws the children into the kitchen, where they cannot tear their eyes away. Could there be any more mysterious daily ritual than eating? It is the unity of life, turning dead things into living bodies. Surely, it's a feast of eternal life made up each day of love and trust.

Sargodha, Punjab, Pakistan, 2011.

자전거를 타고 귀가할 때

예전에는 천국이라 불렸으나

지금은 지옥이라 불리는 땅, 파키스탄.

마중 나온 아이를 태우고 노을길을 달린다.

"오늘도 폭음이 울렸지요.

오늘도 곡절이 많았지요.

그래도 죽지 않고 다치지 않고

아이들 먹을 걸 구해 들고 귀가할 수 있어

오늘도 감사한 날입니다."

지구 위에는 오늘도 살아있음과

일용할 양식을 구해가는 것만으로도

그냥 고맙고 눈물 나는 그런 하루가 있다.

2

GOING HOME BY BICYCLE

It used to be called Paradise, but now it's a land called Hell, Pakistan. He goes speeding along, carrying the child who came out to greet him. "There were explosions again today. There were lots of ups and downs today, too. Still, I did not die, did not get hurt, found something for the kids to eat, and was able to reach home, so today is a day to be grateful for." Just being alive on earth today, just getting one's daily bread, is enough for a day of gratitude and tears.

Sargodha, Punjab, Pakistan, 2011.

짜 이 를 마 시 는 시 간

눈부신 만년설산에 둘러싸인

높고 깊고 고적한 국경마을 가쿠치.

어둠이 내리면 별빛만 눈에 시린데,

여기 삶의 진경은 이제부터다.

집집마다 짜이 끓이는 향기가 번지면

연분홍빛 아몬드 꽃처럼 이야기꽃이 피어난다.

양털을 잣고 자수를 놓고 나무를 깎으며

아빠는 야크를 물어간 늑대를 잡은 이야기,

엄마는 이웃집 결혼 준비를 도운 이야기,

누나는 아프가니스탄 친구와 정세 이야기,

막내는 학교에 새로 온 선생님 이야기.

늘 보는 가족끼리 저리 할 이야기가 많을까.

온몸으로 살아낸 하루는 나만의 이야기를 남긴다.

국경의 밤은 길고 이야기는 끝이 없다.

2

TIME TO DRINK CHAI

Surrounded by dazzling snowy peaks mountains, a high, deep, secluded
frontier town, Gaguch. Once darkness falls, only starlight dazzles the eyes.
Here and now, true scenes of life begin. As the smell of boiling chai fills every
house, conversations blossom like pale pink almond flowers. While spinning
wool and doing embroidery or cutting wood, Dad talks of catching a wolf
who had carried off a yak, Mom talks about helping neighbors prepare for a
wedding, sister talks of her friend in Afghanistan and the situation there, the
youngest talks of a teacher new to the school. There's so much to talk about,
though the family's always together. There remains talk of the day I have spent
so intensely. Night on the border is long, and the stories are endless.

Barsat village, Gaguch, Pakistan, 2011.

SETTING OUT AGAIN AT DAWN

Any who have come a long way will know, any seeking a path today will know, that here is not my abode,* that my own path is calling me. Oh, I am a wanderer between two worlds, a pilgrim ever walking on in search of a path. Every day is a good day. Once again I set out at dawn.

*Adapted from Karl Rahner

Cochamuco, Cusco, Peru, 2010.

다시 길 떠나는 새벽

먼 길을 걸어온 사람은 알리라.
오늘도 길 찾는 사람은 알리라.
여기가 나의 정처가 아님을.*
나만의 다른 길이 부르고 있음을.
아 나는 두 세상 사이의 유랑자.
걸으면서 길을 찾는 순례자.
하루하루가 좋은 날이다.
다시 새벽에 길을 떠난다.

★ 카를 라너Karl Rahner에게 따와 고쳐 씀

전쟁의 레바논에서, 박노해. Park Nohae in the battlefield of Lebanon, 2007.

박노해

1957 전라남도에서 태어났다. 16세에 상경해 낮에는 노동자로 일하고 밤에는 선린상고⟨야간⟩를 다녔다. **1984** 스물일곱 살에 첫 시집『노동의 새벽』을 출간했다. 군사독재 정권의 금서 조치에도 100만 부 가까이 발간된 이 시집은 당시 잊혀진 계급이던 천만 노동자의 목소리가 되었고, 대학생들을 노동현장으로 뛰어들게 하면서 한국 사회와 문단을 충격으로 뒤흔들었다. 감시를 피해 사용한 박노해라는 필명은 '박해받는 노동자 해방'이라는 뜻으로, 이때부터 '얼굴 없는 시인'으로 알려졌다. **1989** 분단된 한반도에서 사회주의를 처음 공개적으로 천명한 ⟨남한사회주의노동자동맹⟩⟨사노맹⟩을 결성했다. **1991** 7년여의 수배생활 끝에 안기부에 체포되면서 처음으로 얼굴을 드러냈다. 24일간의 고문 후 '반국가단체 수괴' 죄목으로 사형이 구형되고 무기징역에 처해졌다. **1993** 독방에서 두 번째 시집『참된 시작』을 출간했다. **1997** 옥중에서 에세이『사람만이 희망이다』를 출간했다. 이 책은 수십만 부가 퍼지며, 그의 몸은 가둘 수 있지만 그의 사상과 시는 가둘 수 없음을 보여주었다. **1998** 7년 6개월의 수감 끝에 석방되었다. 이후 민주화운동 유공자로 복권됐으나 국가보상금을 거부했다. **2000** "과거를 팔아 오늘을 살지 않겠다"며 권력의 길을 뒤로 하고 '생명 평화 나눔'을 기치로 한 비영리 사회운동단체 ⟨나눔문화⟩(www.nanum.com)를 설립했다. **2003** 이라크 전쟁터에 뛰어들면서, 전세계 가난과 분쟁 현장에서 평화활동을 이어왔다. **2010** 낡은 흑백 필름 카메라로 기록해온 사진을 모아 첫 사진전 「라 광야」展과 「나 거기에 그들처

럼」展(세종문화회관)을 열었다. 304편의 시를 엮어 12년 만의 시집『그러니 그대 사라지지 말아라』를 출간했다. **2012** 나눔문화가 운영하는 〈라 카페 갤러리〉에서 박노해 사진전을 상설 개최하고 있다. 파키스탄 사진전「구름이 머무는 마을」, 버마 사진전「노래하는 호수」, 티베트 사진전「남김없이 피고 지고」, 안데스 께로 사진전「께로티카」, 수단 사진전「나일 강가에」, 에티오피아 사진전「꽃피는 걸음」, 볼리비아 사진전「티티카카」, 페루 사진전「그라시아스 알 라 비다」, 알 자지라 사진전「태양 아래 그들처럼」, 인디아 사진전「디레 디레」, 카슈미르 사진전「카슈미르의 봄」, 인도네시아 사진전「칼데라의 바람」, 쿠르드 사진전「쿠르디스탄」, 라오스 사진전「라오스의 아침」, 팔레스타인 사진전「올리브나무의 꿈」 그리고「하루」, 「단순하게 단단하게 단아하게」, 「길」展을 개최했다. 현재 18번째 전시를 이어가고 있으며, 총 30만 명의 관람객이 다녀갔다. **2014** 아시아 사진전「다른 길」展(세종문화회관) 개최와 함께 사진에세이『다른 길』을 출간했다. **2017**『촛불혁명-2016 겨울 그리고 2017 봄, 빛으로 쓴 역사』(감수)를 출간했다. **2020** 첫 번째 시 그림책『푸른 빛의 소녀가』를 출간했다. 감옥에서부터 30년 동안 써온 단 한 권의 책, '우주에서의 인간의 길'을 담은 사상서를 집필 중이다. '적은 소유로 기품 있게' 살아가는 삶의 공동체 〈참사람의 숲〉을 꿈꾸며, 오늘도 시인의 작은 정원에서 꽃과 나무를 심고 기르며 새로운 혁명의 길로 나아가고 있다.

매일 아침, 사진과 글로 시작하는 하루 〈박노해의 걷는 독서〉 parknohae park_nohae

Park Nohae

1957 Park Nohae was born in South Jeolla Province. Park left his hometown and moved to Seoul when he was 16 years old, he worked during daytime and attended the night classes at Seollin Commercial High School. **1984** Park published his first collection of poems, *Dawn of Labor*, that he wrote at the age of twenty-seven. Nearly a million copies of this collection were sold, in spite of the Korean government's ban, and it shook Korean society and the literary world with its shocking emotional power. This book became the voice representing the forgotten class of ten million workers and encouraged college students to go into the laboring world. He decided to take a pen name, "Park Nohae," meaning "liberation of the laborers," in order to avoid the dictatorial government's surveillance on him. From that time, he was called the "faceless poet." **1989** He formed the "South Korean Socialist Workers' Alliance" that made socialism a public issue for the first time in South Korea. **1991** After more than seven years in hiding he was arrested, and thus finally revealed his 'face.' After twenty-four days of investigation with illegal torture, the prosecution demanded the death penalty for the 'leader of an anti-state organizations,' and he was sentenced to life imprisonment. **1993** While he was in prison, a second poetry collection was published, *True Beginning*. **1997** He published a collection of essays, titled *Only a Person is Hope*. This book sold hundreds of thousands of copies, showing that although his body could be imprisoned, his ideas and poems could not be restrained. **1998** He was finally freed after seven years and six months in prison. Thereafter, he was reinstated as a contributor to the democratization movement, but he refused any state compensation. **2000** Park decided to leave the way for power, saying, "I will not live today by selling the past," and he established a nonprofit social movement organization "Nanum Munhwa," meaning "Culture of Sharing," (www. nanum.com) that would have "Life, Peace, and Sharing" as its core values. **2003** Right after the United States' invasion of Iraq, he flew to the field of war. Since then, he has continued to conduct activities aimed at establishing global peace in places of poverty and conflict. **2010** He held his first photo exhibition, titled "Ra Wilderness," and second exhibition "Like them, I am there" at the Sejong Center for the Performing Arts (one of the most significant culture and arts spaces in Seoul). In October, he published a new collection of poems after twelve years, titled *So You Must Not Disappear*, containing three hundred and four poems. **2012** "Ra Cafe Gallery" that "Nanum Munhwa" runs, has been holding permanent exhibitions of Park Nohae. He continues to hold photo exhibitions, and a total of 300,000 visitors have so far visited his exhibitions. **2014** Park held a photo exhibition on Asia, titled "Another Way," and at the same time published his collection of photo essays with the same title, *Another Way*. **2017** He supervised the publication of a book, *The Candlelight Revolution—History written with light-From winter of 2016 to spring of 2017*. **2020** Park published his first poetry picture book, *The Blue Light Girl*. He is writing a book of reflexions, the only such book he has written during the thirty years since prison, "The Human Path in Space." Dreaming of the Forest of True People, a life-community living "a graceful life with few possessions," the poet is still planting and growing flowers and trees in his small garden, advancing along the path toward a new revolution.

Every morning poem with photo, 'Park Nohae's Reading while Walking' parknohae park_nohae

박노해 저서

Books by Park Nohae

길 박노해 사진에세이 03

박노해 시인이 20여 년 동안 기록해온 유랑노트, 「박노해 사진에세이」 시리즈 그 세 번째 책『길』에는 '인간의 길, 시대의 길'에 대한 통찰이 담긴 서문과 14개 나라에서 기록한 37점의 흑백사진이 유장하게 펼쳐지며, 길 찾는 우리에게 뜨거운 용기를 전한다. "길을 잃으면 길이 찾아온다. 길을 걸으면 길이 시작된다. 길은 걷는 자의 것이니."(박노해)

136p | 18,000KRW | 2020

The Path Park Nohae Photo Essay 03

Poet Park Nohae's notes from his past twenty years of wandering. In the series "Park Nohae Photo Essay," the third volume, *The Path*, contains a preface with insights on "the human path, the age's path," and a magnificent spread of thirty-seven black and white photos taken in fourteen countries, offering us heart-warming courage as we seek for a path. "If you lose your way, the path will find you. If you start to walk, the path will begin. The path belongs to the walker."(Park Nohae)

단순하게 단단하게 단아하게

박노해 사진에세이 02

"최고의 삶의 기술은 언제나 가장 단순한 것으로 가장 풍요로운 삶을 꽃피우는 것이니."(박노해) 결핍과 고난 속에서도 단순한 살림으로 풍요롭고, 단단한 내면으로 희망차고, 단아한 기품으로 눈부시게 살아가는 지구마을 사람들의 일상이 37점의 흑백사진과 이야기로 펼쳐진다.

128p | 18,000KRW | 2020

Simply, Firmly, Gracefully

Park Nohae Photo Essay 02

"Surely, life's finest skills, being always the simplest, bring a life of plenty to bloom."(Park Nohae) Productive in simple living despite lack and suffering, full of hope, inwardly robust, gracefully living dazzling lives, the daily lives of inhabitants of the Global Village unfold in thirty-seven black-and-white photos and texts.

그러니 그대 사라지지 말아라

영혼을 뒤흔드는 시의 정수. 저항과 영성, 교육과 살림, 아름다움과 혁명 그리고 사랑까지 붉디 붉은 304편의 시가 담겼다. 인생의 갈림길에서 길을 잃고 헤매는 순간마다 어디를 펼쳐 읽어도 좋은 책. 입소문만으로 이 시집을 구입한 6만 명의 독자가 증명하는 감동. "그러니 그대 사라지지 말아라" 그 한 마디가 나를 다시 살게 한다.

560p | 18,000KRW | 2010

So You Must Not Disappear

The essence of soul-shaking poetry! This anthology of 304 poems as red as its book cover, narrating resistance, spiri-tuality, education, living, the beautiful, revolution and love. Whenever you're lost at a crossroads of your life, it will guide you with any page of it moving you. The intensity of moving is evidenced by the 60,000 readers who have bought this book only through word-of-mouth. "So you must not disappear." This one phrase makes me live again.

노동의 새벽

1984년, 27살의 '얼굴 없는 시인'이 쓴 시집 한 권이 세상을 뒤흔들었다. 독재 정부의 금서 조치에도 100만 부 이상 발간되며 화인처럼 새겨진 불멸의 고전. 억압받는 천만 노동자의 영혼의 북소리로 울려퍼진 노래. "박노해는 역사이고 상징이며 신화다. 문학사적으로나 사회사적으로 우리는 그런 존재를 다시 만날 수 없을지 모른다."(문학평론가 도정일)

172p | 12,000KRW | 2014
30th Anniversary Edition

The Dawn Of Labor

In 1984, an anthology of poems written by 27 years old 'faceless poet' shook Korean society. Recorded as a million seller despite the publication ban under military dictatorship, it became an immortal classic ingrained like a marking iron. It was a song echoing down with the throbbing pulses of ten million workers' souls. "Park Nohae is a history, a symbol, and a myth. All the way through the history of literature and society alike, we may never meet such a being again."(Doh Jeong-il, literary critic)

사람만이 희망이다

34살의 나이에 '불온한 혁명가'로 무기징역을 선고받은 박노해. 그가 1평 남짓한 독방에 갇혀 7년 동안 써내려간 옥중에세이. "90년대 최고의 정신적 각성"으로 기록되는 이 책은, 희망이 보이지 않는 오늘날 더 큰 울림으로 되살아난다. 살아있는 한 희망은 끝나지 않았다고. 다시, 사람만이 희망이라고.

320p | 15,000KRW | 2015

Only A Person Is Hope

Park Nohae was sentenced to life imprisonment as a "rebellious revolutionary" when he was 34 years old. This essay written in solitary confinement measuring about three sq. m. for seven years. This book is recorded as the "best spiritual awakening in the 90s," is born again with the bigger impression today when there seems to be no hope at all. As long as you live, hope never ends. Again, only a person is hope.

다른 길

"우리 인생에는 각자가 진짜로 원하는 무언가가 있다. 분명, 나만의 다른 길이 있다."(박노해) 인디아에서 파키스탄, 라오스, 버마, 인도네시아, 티베트까지 지도에도 없는 마을로 떠나는 여행. 그 길의 끝에서 진정한 나를 만나는 새로운 여행에세이. '이야기가 있는 사진'이 한 걸음 다른 길로 우리를 안내한다.

352p | 19,500KRW | 2014

Another Way

"In our lives, there is something which each of us really wants. For me, certainly, I have my own way, different from others."(Park Nohae) From India, Pakistan, Laos, Burma, Indonesia to Tibet, a journey to villages nowhere to be seen on the map. And a new essay of meeting true self at the end of the road. 'Image with a story' guide us to another way.

푸른 빛의 소녀가 박노해 시 그림책

저 먼 행성에서 찾아온 푸른 빛의 소녀와 지구별 시인의 가슴 시린 이야기. "지구에서 좋은 게 뭐죠?" 우주적 시야로 바라본 우리 삶의 근본 물음. 다가오는 우주시대를 살아갈 아이들의 가슴에 푸른 빛의 상상력을 불어넣는 신비로운 여정. "우리 모두는 별에서 온 아이들. 네 안에는 별이 빛나고 있어."(박노해)

72p | 19,500KRW | 2020

The Blue Light Girl

The poignant tale of paintings of the Blue Light Girl visiting from a distant planet and a poet of Planet Earth. "What is good on Earth?" The fundamental question of our life seen from a cosmic perspective. A mysterious journey inspiring an imagination of blue light in the hearts of the children who will live in the coming space age "We are all children from the stars. Stars are shining in you."(Park Nohae)

하루 박노해 사진에세이 01

초판 5쇄 발행 2021년 1월 18일
초판 1쇄 발행 2019년 10월 16일

사진·글 박노해
편집 김예슬, 윤지영
자문 이기명
번역 안선재
표지 디자인·아트디렉팅 홍동원 표제 글씨 박노해
디자인 조하늘 제작 윤지혜 홍보 이상훈
아날로그 인화 유철수 4도 흑백분판 유화컴퍼니
종이 월드페이퍼 인쇄 경북프린팅
제본 광성문화사 후가공 신화사금박

발행인 임소희
발행처 느린걸음
출판등록 2002년 3월 15일 제300-2009-109호
주소 서울시 종로구 사직로8길 34, 330호
전화 02-733-3773
팩스 02-734-1976
이메일 slow-walk@slow-walk.com
홈페이지 www.slow-walk.com
instagram.com/slow_walk_book

ⓒ 박노해 2019
ISBN 978-89-91418-26-4 04810
ISBN 978-89-91418-25-7 04810(세트)

번역자 안선재(안토니 수사)는 서강대학교 명예교수로
40권 이상의 한국 시와 소설의 영문 번역서를 펴냈다.

One Day Park Nohae Photo Essay 01

First edition, 5th publishing, Jan. 18, 2021
First edition, first publishing, Oct. 16, 2019

Photographed and Written by Park Nohae
Edited by Kim Yeseul, Yun Jiyoung
Directed by Lee Ki-Myoung
Translation by Brother Anthony of Taizé
Art Directed and Cover Designed by Hong Dongwon
Designed by Cho Hanul
Handwritten Title by Park Nohae
Photographic Analogue Prints are by Yu Chulsu
Quadtone Separation by UHWACOMPANY
Print Making by Yun Jihye Marketing by Lee Sanghoon

Publisher Im Sohee
Publishing Company Slow Walking
Address Rm330, 34, Sajik-ro 8-gil, Jongno-gu,
Seoul, Republic of Korea
Tel 82-2-7333773 Fax 82-2-7341976
E-mail slow-walk@slow-walk.com
Website www.slow-walk.com
instagram.com/slow_walk_book

ⓒ Park Nohae 2019
ISBN 978-89-91418-26-4 04810
ISBN 978-89-91418-25-7 04810(SET)

Translator An Sonjae(Brother Anthony of Taizé)
is professor emeritus at Sogang University.
He has published over forty volumes of
translations of Korean poetry and fiction.